Go Ask Ozzie

A Rotten Richie Story

PATRICIA POLACCO

A Paula Wiseman Book
Simon & Schuster Books for Young Readers
New York London Toronto Sydney New Delhi

To Ozzie and in loving memory of my brother, Richard William Barber

SIMON & SCHUSTER BOOKS FOR YOUNG READERS
An imprint of Simon & Schuster Children's Publishing Division
1230 Avenue of the Americas, New York, New York 10020
Copyright © 2021 by Patricia Polacco
All rights reserved, including the right of reproduction in whole or in part in any form.
SIMON & SCHUSTER BOOKS FOR YOUNG READERS is a trademark of Simon & Schuster, Inc.
For information about special discounts for bulk purchases,
please contact Simon & Schuster Special Sales at 1-866-506-1949 or business@simonandschuster.com.
The Simon & Schuster Speakers Bureau can bring authors to your live event.
For more information or to book an event, contact the Simon & Schuster Speakers Bureau
at 1-866-248-3049 or visit our website at www.simonspeakers.com.
Book design by Laurent Linn
The text for this book was set in Chapparel Pro.
The illustrations for this book were rendered in two and six B pencils and acetone markers.
Manufactured in China
0721 SCP
First Edition
10 9 8 7 6 5 4 3 2 1
Library of Congress Cataloging-in-Publication Data
Names: Polacco, Patricia, author.
Title: Go ask Ozzie : a rotten Richie story / Patricia Polacco.
Description: First edition. | New York : Simon & Schuster Books for Young Readers, [2021] | "A Paula Wiseman Book."
| Audience: Ages 4-8. | Audience: Grades 2-3. | Summary: When Patricia starts junior high, her awful older brother
Richie makes her life miserable but after he teaches her to dance she sees that he is not so rotten after all.
Identifiers: LCCN 2020051461 (print) | LCCN 2020051462 (ebook) | ISBN 9781534478558 (hardcover) |
ISBN 9781534478565 (ebook)
Subjects: CYAC: Brothers and sisters—Fiction. | Junior high schools—Fiction. | Schools—Fiction. | Dance—Fiction.
Classification: LCC PZ7.P75186 Go 2021 (print) | LCC PZ7.P75186 (ebook) | DDC [E]—dc23
LC record available at https://lccn.loc.gov/2020051461
LC ebook record available at https://lccn.loc.gov/2020051462

After my bubbie died, we sold our farm in Michigan and moved to California, where Mom got a teaching job in the Oakland public schools. We rented a sweet little house on Russell Street in Berkeley from Mr. Nelson, who owned the laundry right across the alley from us. We were one block off College Avenue. Our neighborhood was called the Elmwood District. It was a bustling place full of friendly people and interesting shops.

Right across College Avenue on the other corner with Russell Street was the Elmwood Pharmacy, flanked by other shops and businesses. The Elmwood Pharmacy was a gathering place for most of the folks that lived in the neighborhood, I think because of Ozzie's lunch counter and soda fountain. Ozzie was magical. Everybody loved him. He always listened to anyone's problems and had the perfect advice for them. And, boy, did I have a problem!

"I don't deserve this!" I wailed as I sat at his counter with my two friends. "What did I do?" I asked as Ozzie leaned in and gave me a knowing grin. "He makes my life *miserable*!" I cried.

My friends nodded in total agreement.

"And, Ozzie, HE STINKS!" I added as I held my nose.

"You can smell him clear down the hall at school!" Sharon added in sympathy.

"He farts with his armpits!" Margie hissed in disgust.

"He never takes a bath either. His feet smell so bad that we almost pass out when he takes off his shoes!" I whined.

"He does everything he can to embarrass us!" Sharon replied.

"He's just plain disgusting!" Margie chirped.

We were all referring to the greatest humiliation of my existence— *my rotten redheaded older brother . . . Richie*!

"One of these days, Ozzie, the doorbell is going to ring at our house, and it will be the *health department*!" I went on.

"I can see it all now," I howled as I stood up dramatically and motioned with a sweeping arm. "Official-looking men will push in and announce that they are *raiding our house because of my brother's room*! And when they open his door, the stench will practically knock them off their feet!

"One of them will say, 'Ma'am . . . we are here by order of the State of California! Your son has broken just about every public health code with the condition of this room!'"

Then I had a drink from my cherry Coke.

"Patricia, with that imagination of yours, you should be a writer! You do tell a good story!" Ozzie laughed as he slapped his knee.

"But, Ozzie, this isn't a story! Do you know what it's like to have to admit to everyone at school that *he*—that *he is my brother*?" I sputtered.

You see, for the past two years I'd been at John Muir Elementary School and, being three years older, Richie had been in junior high. So for a while I'd been safe from scorn. . . . But now this was MY first year at middle school, and it was his last. That meant we were at the *same school again*! Every single day he did something to *mortify me in front of my friends*! Actually, it was a miracle that I even *had* any friends, because of him!

At home it was even worse! Unless Mom forced him into the bathtub, *he didn't go near it*! There were cobwebs on his toothbrush! And he had living things that made their home in his filthy hair! He even had his own flies!

"Patricia," Ozzie said calmly as he patted my hand. "You aren't going to believe this, but someday he'll be your best friend . . . and you'll discover that he isn't as ROTTEN as you think he is!"

I rolled my eyes.

"He's very proud of you. He tells me that you are the best ballet dancer ever! And he's proud of how well you can draw. He's told me all this himself."

I knew Ozzie was trying to make me feel better, and usually he did . . . but I couldn't *imagine ever being glad that Richie was my brother*!

Luckily, Richie wasn't in ANY of my classes. My favorite was art, of course, but I liked music, too. I looked forward to music class because one day each week, instead of learning about music, we had Dart Tinkham give us ballroom dance lessons in the gym.

Since I was good at ballet, you would have thought I would be good at ballroom dancing. But it's very different when you're dancing with another person . . . especially a boy!

This class did give me a reason to be near *Johnnie Pearson*, though. He was the dreamiest, handsomest, most popular boy in our whole grade!

Miss Tinkham let the boys choose their partners for our dancing. . . . *Johnnie never once chose me!*

No, I always got droopy Michael McKennah! The class dweeb . . . geek . . . weirdo! His glasses were so thick that all you could see were his pupils magnified a thousand times. He had a mouth full of wires and braces. . . . He even wore a facebow!

Honestly, I almost wished I were one of the girls who *never* got asked to dance, instead of having to dance with *him*!

One morning a little while later, Mom shook me awake.
Her eyes were wide open as if she had seen something terrible.
"What's wrong, Momma?" I whispered.
Mom told me to get dressed and come in the hallway.
When I got there, she opened the door to my brother's room.
Both of us reeled back in total *disbelief*!
My brother's room was actually clean!
The shock of it was almost too much to bear!

Then the bathroom door suddenly opened and a cloud of steam billowed out into the hallway. *Richie had actually bathed!*

He reeked of Old Spice and pomade hair gel.

But then there was his hair . . . *his hair!*

"How do you like it?" he cooed as he ran his hand along the side of the mountain of hair piled on top of his head and covered in stiff pomade!

"I call it a waterfall in the front"—then he turned around—"and a duck butt in the back," he said proudly as he adjusted the rigid lump of red hair. Mom and I were speechless. Mom said later that she couldn't think of a motherly comment to make . . . and *I certainly couldn't think of anything either!*

For the entire school day, all I could think about was the transformation my brother had undergone.

"Maybe he was abducted by aliens in the middle of the night," Margie said as we walked home after school.

"Or maybe he was replaced in his sleep by his exact double, like in the movie *Invasion of the Body Snatchers*," Sharon suggested.

About then a group of giggling girls ran by us and called back.

"Have you heard?" one said breathlessly. "Ozzie has a new soda jerk! And we hear he is a real dreamboat!" They cooed excitedly as they ran on.

Margie, Sharon, and I looked at one another and ran to Ozzie's to see for ourselves.

The crowd at the counter was HUGE. Girls! All a-dither and aflutter! We fought our way through them and stood waiting to get a glimpse of the boy. His back was to us. . . .

Then he turned around.
I couldn't believe my eyes!
It was him!
It was my rotten redheaded older brother!
It was Richie!

Oh, gag a maggot!
I felt like I couldn't breathe. The room started spinning. . . .
Now I would have to see him at Ozzie's every day!
Oh no!

Then I noticed that Richie was paying particular attention to one of the girls right in front of him!

"He made this especially for me!" she cooed as he set a glass where she was sitting and gave her a wink.

It was Diane Scadutto! My best friend's older sister! Oh, the shame of it all! How was I going to face Sharon from now on?

Yup, my nightmarish existence had just gotten worse!

Apparently they were an ITEM. That's why Richie had cleaned up his act. . . . And he'd gotten a job that most of the boys would have given their right arm to have!

I guess I understood why Ozzie had given my brother the job. Ozzie was like a father to him, and Ozzie liked Richie.

But watching Richie and Diane Scadutto become sweet on each other was more than I could stand! *Puke-a-roooooooo!*

Of course, even though they saw each other all day at school, as soon as Richie got home from the pharmacy, he and Diane were *on the phone*!

For hours at a time!

Mom and I *never got a chance to use the phone almost from that day forward!*

And it was bad enough that I had to see them at school together, but now he was inviting her over for dinner . . . at least once a week!

Whenever she came, I invited Sharon. She was the only person in the world who understood the shame of it all. . . .

Watching them made Sharon and me want to *hurl*!

At school they were just as ridiculous! They *had* to hold hands in the hall, and when they weren't doing that, they were standing by their lockers looking dreamily into each other's eyes. *It was sickening!*

If I hadn't been miserable at school before, I sure was now! He had never had so many kids who wanted to be his friend before!

But even with my brother being the cat's meow, that didn't help to get me noticed by Johnnie Pearson. And I tried everything!

I found out that his favorite color was pink, so for a whole week all I wore was *pink*! Well, *it didn't work!*

Then I found out he liked curly hair! So I wore my hair that way for another whole week! Sleeping in curlers was *awful*! *That didn't work either!*

Then I found out that his favorite lunch at school was tamales! Well, Tuesday was tamale day in the cafeteria. So I loaded my plate with them and sat next to him, hoping he would notice. . . . *Well, he didn't, so I had to eat every last one of them*. . . . I was sick for days!

Then all the posters went up in the hallways at school about the big year-end dance. . . . I realized that this might be my only chance to get Johnnie to notice me.

But my problem was, of course, that I didn't know how to do *any of the dances*. So I took my problem to . . . Who else? . . . Ozzie!

"Ozzie," I wailed. "I watch the local dance party television show every single day and get up and try to do all the dance steps, but I'm not good at it! Ballet is easy for me, but these dances are HARD!"

Ozzie looked at me for a moment.

"*I have to learn these dances. . . . I just have to!* I'm tired of always sitting on the sidelines, a wallflower. *No one asks me to dance!*" I cried.

As Ozzie refilled my cherry Coke, he smiled. "Patricia, I think I have just the thing for you. As it happens, I know one of the best dancers at your school. My wife and I chaperone almost all the school dances, and this kid is terrific!" he sang out.

A glimmer of hope marched across my face.

"I'll bet I could get him to teach you all the latest steps. He can make you one of the most popular girls at the dance!"

I perked up and smiled.

"He and his girlfriend use my storeroom upstairs to practice.
I think he might be there right now!"
"Oh, Ozzie, can I meet him?" I begged.
"Sure. I'll take you up now!"

When Ozzie opened the door to the storeroom, the couple stopped dancing and faced me. . . . I almost *lost my lunch*!

Oh no. . . . It couldn't be! Oh no! It was Richie! Richie and Diane!

I couldn't move! Ozzie went over to them and whispered something. Then they all looked at me!

"So you want to learn the cool stuff, huh, squirt?" my brother said as he came and grabbed my hand. Diane put on a record.

Then he spun me around and lifted me right off my feet!

"Don't look at your feet or mine!" he said as he twirled me around. "Watch my face. . . . *Feel the music.* . . . *You already know that from ballet, so this is almost the same.* . . . *Feel the music!*"

We danced. . . . And we danced. . . . And we danced!

So for the next couple of weeks, Richie and I practiced with Diane. I was happier than happy! *By golly this was going to get me noticed by Johnnie Pearson!*

Then one day Mom told Richie and me that Mr. Nelson, our landlord, had given us notice to move. He had sold the house to the City of Berkeley, and they were going to tear it down to build a fire station.

Even though I was excited about the dance, I was sad about leaving Russell Street, and especially Ozzie!

So Richie and I both took it to Ozzie.

I tried not to cry, but I was fighting back tears.

"I might have just the thing for your family," Ozzie sang out as his eyes lit up. "My cousin is a Realtor. She told me about a house that's coming on the market just down College Avenue on Ocean View Drive, just over the Oakland line. The house is in the Chimes District. The neighborhood's almost exactly like the Elmwood District, *only seven blocks away from here*! They have a theater there too. The Chimes Theater, and they have rock and roll dances every Saturday night!"

Sure enough, that evening Ozzie and his cousin took us all to the Ocean View house. It was as wonderful as he'd said it would be. So many things about it and the neighborhood were like the Elmwood District . . . except Ozzie's. Ozzie's wasn't there!

Mom made an offer on the spot to buy the house. Ozzie's cousin said we would know in a few days if the owners accepted it.

The night of the big dance, we found out that our offer had been accepted and Mom had gotten the house! We were thrilled, but I was even more thrilled at the thought that I would see Johnnie Pearson and at long last *impress him*!

The gym looked *fabulous*. It was decorated like outer space! Stars and planets and the moon hung overhead.

Richie and Diane went off and started to dance.

I took my seat with some of the other girls who were waiting for a boy to come over and pick them.

One after another, each girl got picked, but not me. I was a *wallflower*! Then I saw him . . . *Johnnie Pearson*. He started to walk right toward me. My heart almost stopped in my chest.

He smiled at me . . . *at me*! Then he put his hand out . . . and I reached for it . . . only to see him take Neenonne Palmer by the hand and lead her onto the dance floor. *My heart was broken!*

I fought back tears. All that practicing . . . all that hard work . . . all of those dreams . . .
No one wanted to dance with me! Not even that dud Michael McKennah.

I was MORTIFIED!

Suddenly I felt a hand tugging me right out of my chair! The music started to *boom*!

Shama lama ding dong . . . Ooooorama lama ding dong . . . Shaaaaaa na na na . . .

Richie pulled me to my feet! Then we did all the dances we'd practiced. . . . *The walk.*
The jitterbug. The mashed potato. The chicken. The hully gully. The boogaloo. The shuffle.

We rocked that gym!

Pretty soon everyone else on the dance floor stopped dancing and surrounded us, clapping to the music. We strutted our stuff! Richie threw me up . . . around . . . through . . . and beside him.

Then he threw me straight up into the air. . . . I was flying. . . . I was *airborne. . . . I was flying above all those kids. . . .*

Then I came down and landed in the waiting arms of what was supposed to be my brother. . . .

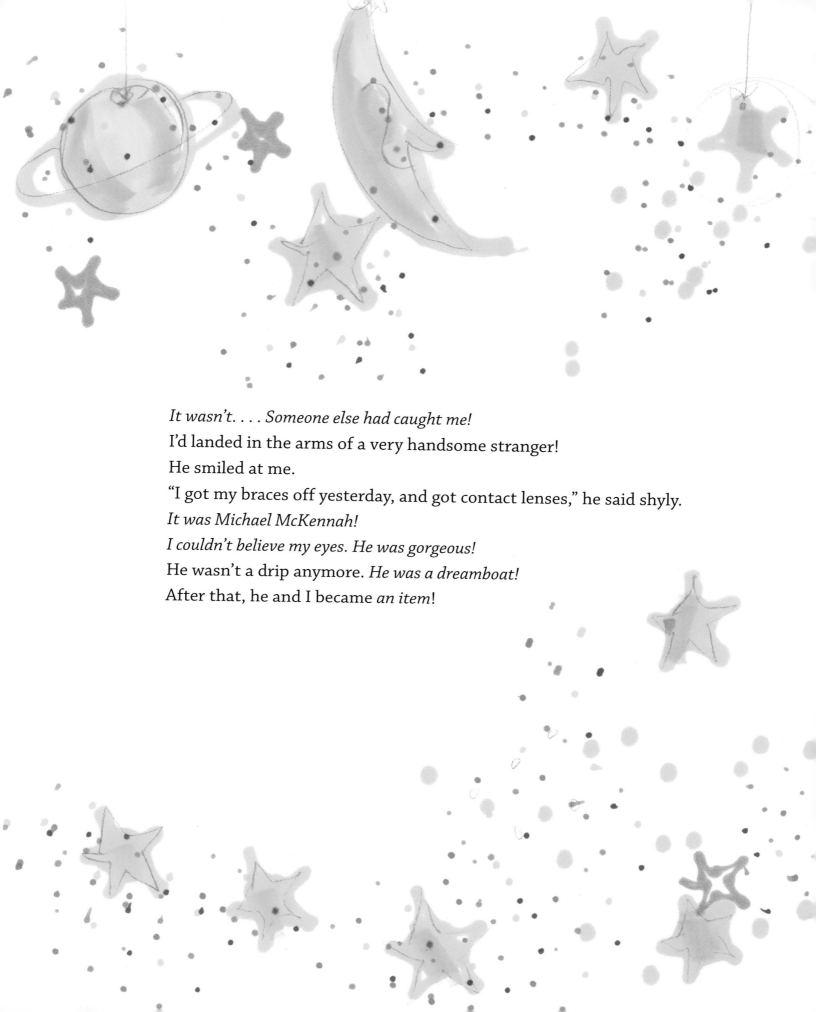

It wasn't. . . . Someone else had caught me!

I'd landed in the arms of a very handsome stranger!

He smiled at me.

"I got my braces off yesterday, and got contact lenses," he said shyly.

It was Michael McKennah!

I couldn't believe my eyes. He was gorgeous!

He wasn't a drip anymore. *He was a dreamboat!*

After that, he and I became *an item*!

AUTHOR'S NOTE

It's hard to believe that wondrous night was almost sixty-five years ago! A café, Baker & Commons, and a bookstore, Mrs. Dalloway's Literary and Garden Arts, now occupy the space where the Elmwood Pharmacy once was. But Ozzie's soda fountain still remains to this day! Ozzie lived to be ninety years old! And his spirit still lingers there.

My brother worked for Ozzie until he graduated from high school. Then Rich joined the air force, probably because of all the adventuresome stories Ozzie had told him about being a pilot in the Second World War. Rich did four tours of duty and upon leaving the service went to live in Northern California in a geodesic dome, where he and his wife raised eight beautiful children!

Mom lived in our family home on Ocean View Drive for almost fifty years, until her death in 1996. We wouldn't have gotten that house if it hadn't been for Ozzie.

As for me, well, I guess Ozzie knew it all those years ago. Telling stories is in my blood, and I became a children's author and illustrator. I have written more than 160 books!

My two grown children still live in the Bay Area. I travel from my farm in Michigan to see them often and especially love seeing my two grandchildren.

When I go for a visit, I always make my way to the corner of College Avenue and Russell Street in the Elmwood District to visit Ozzie's. It's full of people celebrating life. Ozzie would have loved this!

I walk up to the counter and lightly brush its surface with my fingers. As I do, I swear I can still see Ozzie standing behind the counter with one leg hiked up, a pencil behind his ear . . . leaning in and listening to a group of animated young people. . . .

Then he looks at me . . . smiles and winks. My heart fills with joy! How lucky Rich, my mother, and I were to have known him! He changed our lives, as he did for so many.

And like I said at the beginning, he was right about everything, especially that my brother wasn't so rotten after all. . . .

Patricia Polacco

"The Last Sandwich," 1989. Photo: Richard Nagler

"Three Ozzie Generations: Ozzie, Robin Richardson, and Michael Hogan," 2006.
Photo: Richard Nagler